Chief Hawah's
book of Native American
Indians

Chief Hawah's
Book of
Native American Indians

Illustrated by Chris Brown

MARION BOYARS
CHILDREN'S

Published in Great Britain and the United States in 2006 by
MARION BOYARS PUBLISHERS LTD
24 Lacy Road, London SW15 1NL
www.marionboyars.co.uk

Distributed in Australia and New Zealand by Peribo Pty Ltd
58 Beaumont Road, Kuring-gai, NSW 2080

Printed in 2006
10 9 8 7 6 5 4 3 2 1
© Chris Brown 2006
All rights reserved.

A CIP catalogue record for this book is available from the British Library.
A CIP catalog record for this book is available from the Library of Congress.

ISBN 0-7145-3308-4
13 digit ISBN 978-0-7145-3308-7

Set in Bembo 20/24 pt and printed in China.

CONTENTS

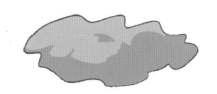

Greetings! My name is Chief Hawah, mighty leader of the Sioux tribe from the central plains of North America.

My people have lived in America as hunters and warriors for thousands of years, long before anyone from Europe came to these lands and drove us away from our homes. But did you know that some of us are also shamans and sorcerors, in contact with the spirit world?

There is much for everyone to learn about the customs of the
Native American Indians and their traditional way of life.

Different Tribes

There are lots of different tribes of Indians and they all speak different languages. These are some of the main tribes:

The **Sioux** were one of the most famous tribes – and perhaps the largest – who inhabited the vast Northern Plains region of the American West.

The **Seminole** tribe lived in the swamps of Florida and were divided into eight camps called Panther, Bear, Deer, Wind, Bigtown, Bird, Snake and Otter. They could be spotted by the distinctive headbands they wore.

The name 'red indian' comes from the **Beothuk** tribe, who used to paint their bodies and faces red with a special dye. Some people use the term for all American Indians, but this is wrong as the Beothuk tribe were the only ones who painted themselves red – allegedly to protect themselves from insects.

It was the **Apache** community who dominated the Texan borders and were known for their superior fighting skills during warfare. The name 'Apache' means 'fighting men' and the warriors used to wear masks made of buckskin.

Hunting and Weapons

The Hunt

Traditionally, the women remained near the campsite, concentrating on growing crops and raising children whilst the men went on dangerous hunts for buffalo.

When a young boy was old enough, his father would let him join the hunt, usually after a special ceremony round the fire.

If the boy performed a great feat like touching an enemy during battle or stealing his horse he would be honoured by the whole tribe.

Weapons

The usual weapons were axes, spears, clubs and the bow and arrow, which the Native American Indians were particularly skilled at using. This formed their main defence against the guns that settlers used when trying to invade their territories.

Lifestyle and Dress

On the move...

Many Native American Indians were nomadic people, who would move from place to place depending on where they could find a good area for hunting, or water from the rivers or lakes. To help them move around easily they would live in special tents called 'wigwams' and 'tepees', which they could pack up and move whenever they wanted.

Horses, the travois and canoes

To transport goods the Native American Indians would use a cart without wheels made from the branches of a tree called a 'travois', which they dragged along the ground. If they were near to a river though, they would use canoes. Have you ever tried to paddle upstream in a canoe — it's not as easy as you think!

Clothes

The Native American Indian style of dress is very distinctive. Along with shoes called 'moccasins', the men would wear heavy duty trousers made from cattle skin and stitched at the sides. The women wore dresses, also made from animal skin or cloth. Both men and women decorated their clothes with beads and embroidery.

War Bonnets

The bravest warriors often wore a giant headdress or 'war bonnet' made from eagle feathers and decorated with beads or precious stones. These might also be worn for special ceremonies, like the one before the hunt.

Shamans and Sorcerors

Native American Indians have always been thought of as highly spiritual, often possessing great wisdom. The elders of the tribe were admired for their remarkable knowledge of herbal remedies and would sometimes use potions made from herbs to gain visions of the supernatural world.

Totem poles
Ceremonies and ritual dances would traditionally take place around the totem pole, which was a giant wooden sculpture carved with masked faces and sometimes outstretched eagle wings at the top.

Visions

Visions played an important role in the spiritual beliefs of many Native American Indians, and those tribes living on the plains also had witch doctors called 'shamans' or medicine men who performed healing rituals. Their chief ritual was the sun dance at summer solstice.

Torture tests
The warriors of some communities practised gruelling torture tests in return for supernatural assistance; the Mandan tribe, for example, hung themselves from pegs skewered under the skin. Frightening!

The Dreamcatcher

The elders taught that dreams of great power float around at night looking for people to dream them. They would place a 'dreamcatcher' made of wicker and feathers above people's beds which was supposed to trap any bad dreams, entangling them in its woven web until they'd disappear at daybreak. Only the good dreams, which knew the way, would be let through and guided gently to the sleeping ones…

Famous Native American Indians

Hiawatha

Hiawatha was the legendary Mohawk who lived in isolation as a vagabond until a spirit guide appeared to make him change his ways. From then on he travelled amongst his people, the Iroquois, spreading a message of peace and preaching that all tribes should end their violent ways and stop fighting each other.

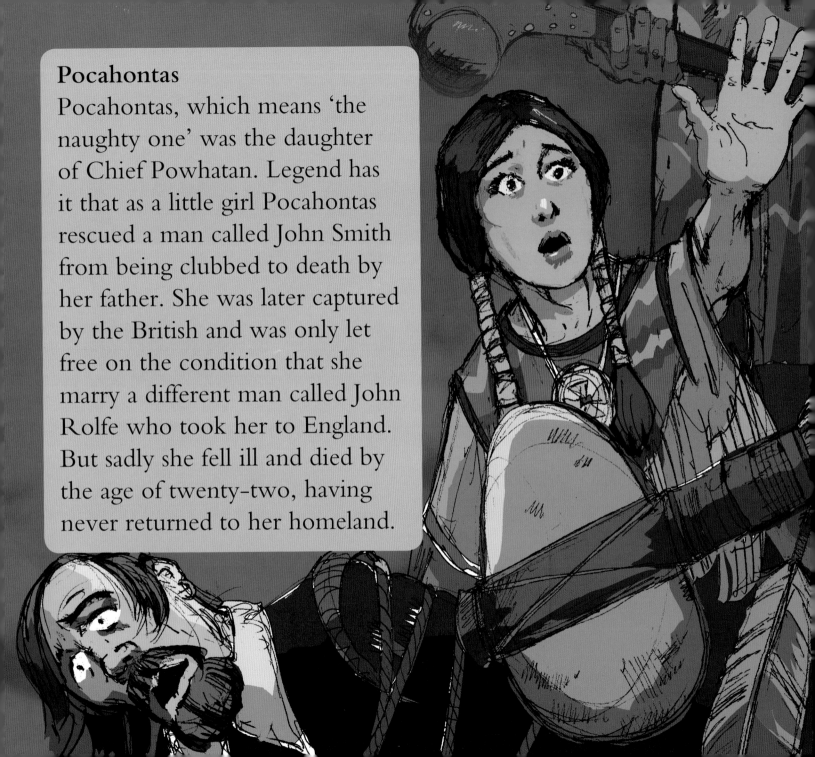

Pocahontas

Pocahontas, which means 'the naughty one' was the daughter of Chief Powhatan. Legend has it that as a little girl Pocahontas rescued a man called John Smith from being clubbed to death by her father. She was later captured by the British and was only let free on the condition that she marry a different man called John Rolfe who took her to England. But sadly she fell ill and died by the age of twenty-two, having never returned to her homeland.

Geronimo

Geronimo was one of the last Apache leaders to give in to the American invaders. Because he fought against all the odds and held out for so long, holed up in the Sierra Madre Mountains in Mexico, he became famous for his courage. In the end it took 5,000 soldiers, one-quarter of the entire army, 500 scouts and up to 3,000 Mexican soldiers to track him down. His reputation spread so far that to this day people all around the world call out 'Geronimo!' when they are about to perform daring feats.

Yellow Thunder

Some leaders, like Yellow Thunder of the Winnebago tribe, were tricked into signing away their lands without knowing it and were told they had to leave. In 1837, Yellow Thunder travelled all the way to Washington, to demand that the President give back his ancestors' homeland, but the President wouldn't listen.

So Yellow Thunder and the Winnebagos refused to move. When the troops arrived, Yellow Thunder was captured and held in chains, but the other chiefs realized if they resisted their people would be killed and decided to co-operate. It was only much later, as an old man, that Yellow Thunder finally returned to his homeland, to run a farm with his wife.

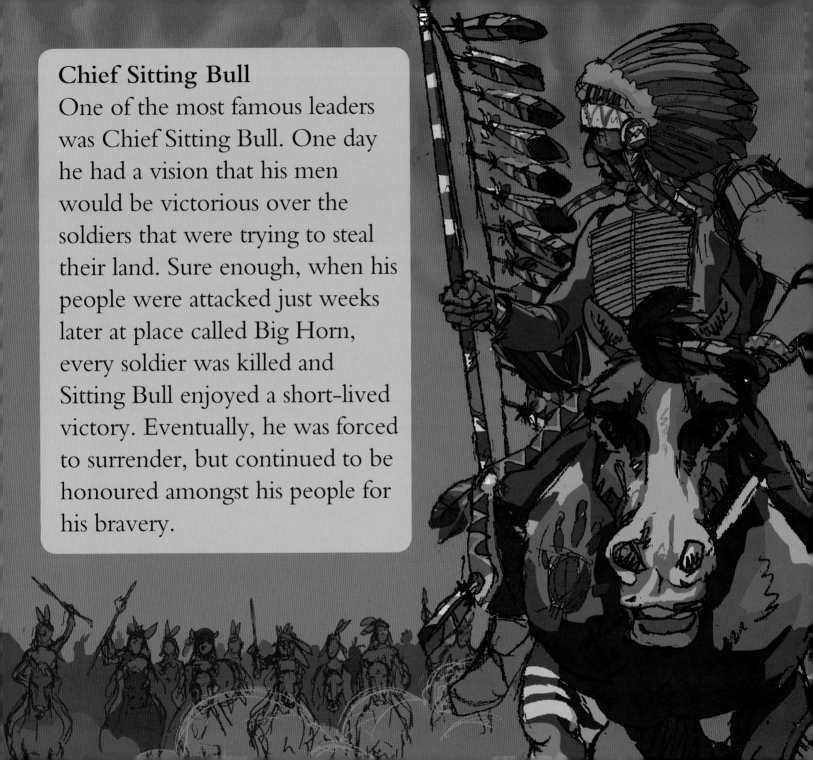

Chief Sitting Bull

One of the most famous leaders was Chief Sitting Bull. One day he had a vision that his men would be victorious over the soldiers that were trying to steal their land. Sure enough, when his people were attacked just weeks later at place called Big Horn, every soldier was killed and Sitting Bull enjoyed a short-lived victory. Eventually, he was forced to surrender, but continued to be honoured amongst his people for his bravery.

DID YOU KNOW THAT...

For Native American Indians the bald eagle is the most sacred of all birds. Turtles are also considered to have a special purpose and turtle shells were worn by the women of a tribe called the Cherokees during ceremonial dances.

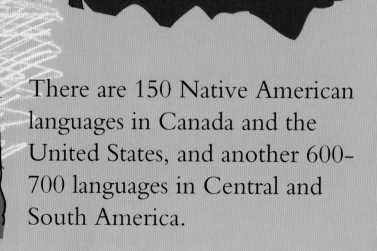

There are 150 Native American languages in Canada and the United States, and another 600–700 languages in Central and South America.

Although Native American Indian tradition claims that their people have always inhabited the USA, most of the scientific evidence suggests that they came to America from Asia in prehistoric times, which would have been over 20,000 years ago. (It is hard to keep records from so long ago, so perhaps both are right!)

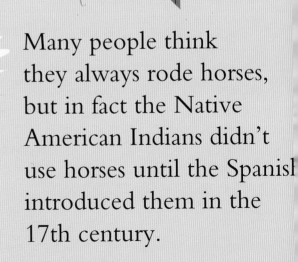

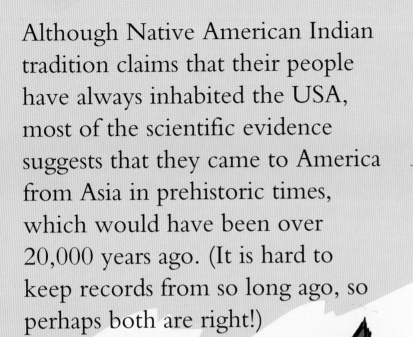

Many people think they always rode horses, but in fact the Native American Indians didn't use horses until the Spanish introduced them in the 17th century.

Native American Indian women used to carry their children in a special harness called a 'Papoose'. I bet this was hot for the babies when they were on desert plains!

Lots of the most interesting place names in the USA have come from the Native American Indian language. For example, 'Idaho' in Indian means 'gem of the mountains' and 'Mississippi' means 'great river'.

QUICK FUN QUIZ

1. What did the Native American Indians use to transport goods from place to place? a) Gypsy wagons b) Primitive types of cars c) A special kind of cart with no wheels called a 'travois'.

2. What did the Apache tribe wear on their faces when in battle? a) Sunglasses – they liked the fashion b) Make-up to distract their opponents c) A mask made of buffalo skin.

3. What did the Mandan tribe do as torture tests? a) Make their members walk over burning coals b) Hang them up with pegs skewered under the skin c) Dunk their heads under water until they choke.

4. Which famous warrior's name is still used as an outcry before performing daring feats? a) Geromino! b) Yellow Thunder! c) Pocahontas!

5. What were the medicine men or witch doctors of any given tribe called? a) Elders b) Dreamcatchers c) Shamans.

6. What did the Native American Indians hunt? a) Buffalo b) Desert coyote c) Long horn cattle.

7. What does the name Pocahontas mean? a) The lively one b) The cheeky one c) The naughty one.

8. What is a Totem Pole? a) A long wooden pole used to hang the washing from b) A giant carved sculpture used for ceremonial dance c) A weapon that only the most fearsome warriors could use.

9. Which animal shells did the Cherokee women wear? a) Turtle shells b) Tortoise shells c) Terrapin shells.

10. Which Chief eventually managed to return to his homeland, to run a farm with his wife? a) Sitting Bull b) Yellow Thunder c) Haiwatha.

(Answers: 1 = c, 2 = c, 3 = b, 4 = a, 5 = c, 6 = a, 7 = c, 8 = b, 9 = a, 10 = b.)

I hope that you enjoyed learning about the Native American Indians and are inspired to find out more. That's all for now, until we meet again – so long!